S0-ARC-776

"Let's camp out overnight!" Timmy Tiger said to his
brother, Tommy. "That would be fun!" replied Tommy.
"Let's ask Mother if we may spend the night in the jungle."

"You may camp out tonight, but don't go too far away,"
their mother warned. "The jungle has many dangerous
animals. You may find trouble if you go too far."

"Oh, we won't go too far," promised Timmy. "We'll
be careful and watch out for any big animals in the jungle.
Come on, Tommy, let's pack!"

3

Timmy and Tommy packed their tent
and some clothes in their overnight bags. They
also packed some food. Before they left,
their mother gave them a big box of freshly baked
sugar cookies.

4

Timmy and Tommy started for the jungle.
After a short time they came to a clearing
with a big shady tree.

"This looks like a good place to put up
our tent,"
Timmy said. "Let's camp here."

5

"No, Timmy. We can rest here, but let's go just a little farther," answered Tommy. "If we are going to camp out overnight, let's go into the jungle."

Timmy and Tommy rested in the cool shade under the big tree. Soon, they were on their way again. They reached the jungle, and forgetting their mother's warning, they wandered deep inside.

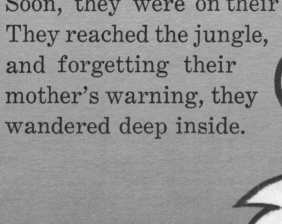

Far into the jungle, Timmy and Tommy found a large tree by a brook. "Let's camp under this tree," Timmy said. Timmy and Tommy put their tent by the brook under the tree.

"We'll unpack later. Let's explore!" shouted Timmy excitedly.

Timmy and Tommy set out to explore the jungle. They explored nests and holes and caves.

"This is fun!" yelled Tommy. "I like exploring the jungle."

"Look!" cried Timmy. "Look on that tree trunk. There's a sign. It reads, 'Wanted, the Masked Bandit. Reward!'"

"A Masked Bandit! Maybe we better go home and camp in our own backyard," Tommy said. "Go home now? Not me!" replied Timmy. "Maybe we can catch the Masked Bandit and collect the reward. Won't Mother be proud of us!"

WANTED
THE
MASKED
BANDIT
REWARD

"Let's build a trap for the Masked Bandit," said Timmy
"If he comes near our tent we can catch him!"

Timmy and Tommy stretched a rope between two trees
near one of the holes they had explored.

"The rope will trip the Masked Bandit," Timmy said.
"Now let's make the hole look just like the traps that me
use to catch animals for the circus and zoo."

Timmy and Tommy spread branches and sticks over the
hole. Then they spread grass over the branches and sticks.

"See, Tommy, it doesn't even look like a hole," Timmy said proudly. "When the Masked Bandit trips over the rope, he will fall into the hole. Then we can collect the reward!"

That night Timmy and Tommy snuggled in their bed inside the tent. They listened to the animals in the jungle. They heard howling and squawking and trumpeting and bellowing.

A big, black screech owl in the tree
overhead hooted, "Hoo Hoo, Hoo Hoo, Hoo Hoo!"

Tommy whispered to his brother, "Timmy, are you scared?"

"Scared? Not yet," Timmy answered. "Not as long as the big animals stay away from our tent!" Timmy and Tommy quietly lay side by side with their eyes wide open listening to all the strange sounds. "Do you hear anythin on top of our tent?" Tommy whispered.

"No, I don't hear anything," Timmy answered, unsure. "Listen! Somebody is crawling around o top of our tent!" repeated Tommy. Timm listened. Yes, there was a sound coming from the top of the tent!

Thump! Thump! Thump!

Timmy and Tommy whispered at the same time, "What
f it is the Masked Bandit!"

Thump! Thump! Thump! The thumping came closer and
loser.

Thump! Thump! Thump! Timmy and Tommy saw a
hadow in the doorway of their tent. "Look! It's the
Iasked Bandit!" Timmy whispered excitedly. Timmy and
ommy were almost afraid to breathe.   15

Timmy and Tommy could
see the dark form of the
Masked Bandit thump into their
tent. Then two black hands
emptied everything out of the
overnight bags, leaving them
upside down.

When the Masked Bandit stopped and
looked around the tent, Timmy and Tommy pulled
their covers over their heads. Their hearts beat fast as
they heard the Masked Bandit open jars and upset cans!

Timmy and Tommy peeked out from under the covers. The Masked Bandit had found the box of freshly baked sugar cookies that Timmy and Tommy's mother had baked for their camping trip!

"Tommy," whispered Timmy, "what should we do? We can't let him eat our sugar cookies!"

At that moment the Masked Bandit saw Timmy and Tommy. He pulled back the covers! Timmy and Tommy now clearly saw the black mask over the bandit's eyes!

"RUN!" yelled Tommy. Timmy and Tommy leaped out of bed and ran from their tent! Tommy looked back and saw the Masked Bandit close behind!

"Run toward the rope we stretched in front of the hole," cried Timmy. "We will trap the Masked Bandit!" They ran as fast as they could, but the Masked Bandit was gaining! "Faster! Faster!" panted Timmy. "We are almost to the rope and the hole!"

19

Timmy and Tommy were running so fast that when they reached the trap, Tommy tripped over the rope they had strung for the bandit! Over he fell, into the hole!

"Help! Help!" cried Tommy. "I'm in the hole. Save me, Timmy!"

Timmy had no time to decide. "Oh, my! Tommy's caught and the Masked Bandit is almost here! I must hide and think of a plan!" thought Timmy to himself. Timmy hid behind a bush. His heart was pounding so hard he thought the Masked Bandit would hear him! "I must do something!" he thought. "I must save Tommy from the Masked Bandit!" Timmy peeked out from behind the bush and saw the dark form of the Masked Bandit looking down at Tommy from the edge of the hole. "Timmy, Timmy, where are you?" Tommy cried. "Hurry! Do something!"

The Masked Bandit stood over the hole, holding the box of freshly baked sugar cookies and waiting for Tommy.

"Don't worry, Tommy!" Timmy shouted. "I'll think of something!" Timmy started racing back toward the tent. The Masked Bandit saw Timmy and ran after him. Timmy ran and ran. He was almost out of breath when he saw one of the caves he and his brother had explored earlier in the day. Panting hard and not knowing what to do, Timmy hid inside the cave.

The Masked Bandit looked into the cave. Timmy flattened himself against the wall of the cave and held his breath. At last the Masked Bandit gave up looking for Timmy. He left the cave and went back to the hole where Tommy was trapped.

Timmy fearfully peeked out of the cave. With the Masked Bandit gone, he raced toward the tent again. His legs were tired but he couldn't stop now. He knew he had to do something to rescue his brother from the Masked Bandit, and he must do it quickly! Tired and panting, Timmy reached the tent. He pulled a sheet off the bed and started racing to the hole again. "I must get Tommy out of the trap before the Masked Bandit harms him," thought Timmy. Faster and faster he ran! His heart pounded harder and harder. Finally, Timmy reached the hole. He tiptoed behind the Masked Bandit. Just as he was ready to throw the sheet over him, the Masked Bandit turned around!

23

The Masked Bandit started after Timmy. Timmy ran and ran, up and down the jungle, back and forth, with the Masked Bandit close behind.

Timmy ran toward the rope. When he reached the rope he jumped over it just in time! The Masked Bandit ran into the rope so hard, it threw him backwards. He stumbled and crashed to the ground! Timmy quickly threw the sheet over the Masked Bandit and tied the corners together.

Using the rope from between the two trees, Timmy pulled Tommy from the hole to safety.

"Thanks, Timmy. I knew you'd think of something!"
Tommy told his brother. "Mother was right!" said Timmy.
"There is danger in the jungle! But now what shall we do
with the Masked Bandit?" The Masked Bandit struggling
inside the white sheet heard Timmy. "Please," he
26   cried, "let me out of here. I won't harm you."

"But you are the Masked Bandit. We can't let you go," Timmy replied. "Me? But I am not a bandit," cried the struggling figure. "Let me out and I will prove to you that I am not the Masked Bandit!"

Cautiously, Timmy and Tommy untied the corners of the sheet.

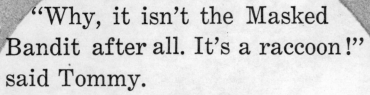

"Why, it isn't the Masked Bandit after all. It's a raccoon!" said Tommy.

"Why did you think I was the Masked Bandit?" the raccoon asked.

"Because in the dark tent, all we could see was the black mask you are wearing," Timmy and Tommy told the raccoon.

"This isn't a mask," the raccoon replied. "It just looks
if I am wearing a mask because my fur is black
ound my eyes." "But why did you go through our
nt and turn everything upside down?" asked Timmy.
"I was looking for something sweet to eat. I thought the
nt was deserted," the raccoon meekly answered. "I
asn't going to harm anybody." "Then why did you
ase us?" asked Tommy. "After I found you, I wanted
explain and return the sugar cookies I took, but you
mped up and ran so fast I didn't have a chance. I'm
ally sorry if I scared you," said the raccoon.

"I guess we did leave in a hurry," agreed Timmy and Tommy. "Look. Here are the sugar cookies. Would you like to share them with us?" Timmy and Tommy asked the raccoon.

Timmy, Tommy, and the raccoon sat down together and ate all the sugar cookies.

"Would you like to come home with us?" Timmy asked the raccoon. "Mother will give you all the sugar cookies you want."